PLAY IT FILTHY

KINGS OF THE TOWER BOOK 4

MAY SAGE

CHAPTER 1

"Mr. Ashworth. Welcome to New York."

Ed glanced at the executive assistant sent by his American headquarters and inwardly groaned. Another model-type with long nails and tons of makeup. He doubted she could type at a decent speed. Why was it that everyone assumed that he was more interested in his employees' proficiency with their tongues than in their efficiency?

He could be wrong. Maybe she was pretty *and* smart.

"Any news on the Kings deal?" he asked her.

The assistant stumbled to open her bag and pull out a tablet. Starting it up took her a whole three minutes. His driver had arrived by the time she said, "Kings? We have an email from King Industries from yesterday... hang on, let me read it." He tried not to let his annoyance show, because he was going to have to work with the girl until he found a decent replacement.

"Please do. In silence."

He got in the car and checked his own messages, definitely rattled. Edmund Ashworth wasn't one to let things rattle him, but he had to admit: Hester was getting on his nerves. Quite an achievement for a little old lady he'd never even seen. He had started a simple transaction that should have been completed within seventy-two hours a month ago, and he still wasn't any closer to buying the harbor he needed. Bloody hell, they'd warned him that doing business with the Kings wasn't easy, but he had imagined power struggles in the boardroom. That hadn't made him flinch. Fucking businesses was what he did. Ed had never thought that he'd get cock-blocked by a crone before he'd even gotten to first base.

"The email says that Mr. Desmond King is

currently unavailable, except for emergencies."

He tapped his armrest impatiently. From one corner of the world to the next, a meeting with him was considered an emergency. Who the fuck did those Kings think they were to dismiss him like that for a whole fucking month? "Who signed the email?"

"A Hester Hall, sir."

That twat again. She was seriously getting on his nerves. Some nobody called Hester shouldn't have that much power over a man like Desmond King's schedule. "Try to go around her. She's got something against me personally." He didn't think they'd ever come across each other, but he had no other explanation as to why the deal was still not going through. The driver started the car, and they left the private airport, heading toward the center of the city. Ed was a London man through and through, but he did love the energy in NYC. He wasn't exactly here for a leisure trip, but he'd try to make the best of it.

"To the Trent residence, sir?" the driver asked through the intercom. "No, directly to the lawyer." He had an estate to settle, and a huge family of vipers to deal with. If he could manage that in a couple of weeks and close the King deal, he'd be on his way back to Europe in time for his grandmother's birthday. God knew Cici Trent would have his balls if he didn't make it.

The driver joined the New York traffic, and they advanced at a snail's pace. Ed's fault for arriving in the middle of the day, but he hadn't had much choice in the matter. One does not schedule a trip like this one in advance.

His great uncle, Malcolm Trent, was one of the only people he could stand from his grandmother's side of the family. The man had been smart, funny, and, unlike most of the Trents, kind. He'd struggled since his stroke, and his passing, though deeply affecting Edmund, hadn't been a surprise, or even a sorrowful event. He'd hated to see the man suffer.

For a time, Malcolm had stayed in Fairweather, the Ashworths' land in northern England, but the Trents had bullied him into going to a luxurious care facility in upstate New York a year ago. Ed knew it wasn't out of concern for his well-being. When Edward Trent passed away thirty years ago, Malcolm had inherited a share of his father's company, like all of the nine Trent children, Cici included. Edward's will had been written in a way that obliged the beneficiary to keep ten percent of their inheritance in a trust for their children and grandchildren. A trust managed by a third party.

The nine Trent ancients had gotten about a billion apiece, but there was a large chunk they'd just had to sit on, unable to get their greedy paws on it. The trusts were only passed to the children when they got married, as per Edward's stipulation. The man had fought in both World Wars, for heaven's sake; it wasn't a surprise that he'd been so old-fashioned.

Almost all of Edward's children had had at least two kids of their own, and those two kids popped out two or three children each. There were hundreds of thousands held in trust. Cici didn't give two shits about her father's money; she'd married Edmund's granddad, an Englishman with lands and a title. The rest of her siblings were another matter.

Malcolm was the exception in the large Trent litter. Unlike the rest of them, he never married, and never fathered any children. He had access to his entire inheritance, and he'd invested it wisely.

Malcolm wasn't an asshole; he'd given his siblings jobs when they'd needed them, cuts of his company's profits, allowances. They'd always acted like ungrateful assholes entitled to it. Malcolm hadn't even been invited to his own niece's wedding fifteen years ago, because he'd come out of the closet, and introduced his boyfriend the year before that.

The Trents had never been Ed's favorite people, but the event created a real divide in the family. He'd been twenty-two at the time, old enough to take a stand. From that point onward, he hadn't even spoken to anyone using that last name, save for his uncle.

The stroke hadn't changed anything. The Trents continued to ignore Malcolm. When his boyfriend died, they didn't so much as send a sympathy card.

About a year ago, Malcolm's doctor had told them that they needed to get ready; his body and mind were failing him. He didn't have long to live.

Edmund didn't know how the Trents heard of that, but they closed in on the sick old man, involving lawyers, sending investigators, doctors, until the poor old guy cracked, telling them he'd go to New York. They claimed the Ashworths were only taking care of him to get to his fortune. Yeah, right. Like Ed, or anyone in his family, needed it. They'd wanted to get their paws on him in his final hours and peek at his will.

About sixteen hours ago, the call Ed had dreaded for months had come during the night. Ten hours later, after working through the night to settle every important document on his desk, he was on the first flight to NYC.

He was named executor of Malcolm's will, so it was time to see if the Trents had gotten their wish.

CHAPTER 2

Hester wasn't much of a homebody. She lived in a modern, luxurious, and spacious NYC building free of charge, courtesy of her high-powered position in King Industries, but as excited as she had been about it when she'd first started this job, five years later, she had to admit that she hated the place. It was sterile—a chrome and glass clinic. She wasn't allowed to paint walls, change the carpets, or basically do anything that might have added some life into the place. So she just slept there, and spent her time elsewhere.

Waking up at five-thirty, she stumbled to the bathroom and brushed her teeth before grabbing her gym bag and heading right to work.

It was a short walk from the employee apartment to the Kings and Knights Tower, Desmond King's base of operations.

"Hi, Bruno."

"Miss Hall," the night security guard greeted her. "It's quiet today."

"Good, thank you."

She wasn't that much of a workaholic that she'd head to work by six; at least, not when she didn't have a pressing project on her plate. Instead of heading to her office, Hester took an elevator underground to the gym.

She started with a leisurely swim before going for a quick run, attending a yoga class, and enjoying a long shower.

The gym was state-of-the-art, like everything else owned by the Kings. Any employee in this building could use it, but she was one of the only ones who could boast of having her own changing room, with a spa and a mini bar. One of the many benefits of being Desmond King's executive assistant.

At eight, Hes got dressed and headed up to the penthouse.

"Miss Hall."

"Good morning, Chris," she said, greeting her own assistant with a warm smile. "You're early."

"So are you."

Neither of them technically started before nine. How sad that two twenty-somethings showed up an hour early at work most days. Except when she looked at her bank account's balance. Then it wasn't sad at all.

"Did you have a chance to look at today's schedule?"

"Not many changes; Slate asked if they could be seen at five rather than twelve. I said yes on your behalf; hope you don't mind."

"Of course not."

Especially not for a partner as important as William Slate.

“Great initiative. Anything else?"

"Another email from Ashworth," Chris said with a grimace.

Hes sighed.

Ashworth. The self-important Brit who wanted to buy—and no doubt destroy—one of their harbors in southern Italy.

He wasn't someone she could ignore, even if she'd wanted to, so Hes had reported his offer to Desmond immediately. Des had been clear: his priority was Ryn right now, at the end of her pregnancy. No harbor was worth his time. He'd given Hes full power to do as she pleased with the situation.

Hes had contacted Ashworth, telling him she'd meet him to discuss the specifics. She'd even offered to fly to London, something she didn't do for just anyone. But Ashworth wouldn't deal with anyone except Desmond King.

Hes knew what she'd signed up for from the beginning: a career in this industry meant dealing with misogynistic pricks on a daily basis. But there was something in his tone that seriously set her teeth on edge.

Hester had read his first email back so many times she knew it by heart. She recited it to herself when she was hitting her punching bag.

"Dear Hester,

I don't think you understand the situation. I, Edmund Ashworth the Second, owner of Ashworth Incorporated, wish to speak to your employer, Desmond King. Desmond King. No one else.

Kindly arrange this meeting.

Regards,

Ed."

Her jaw set, she headed inside her corner office and zeroed in on her computer. The lights turned on as she advanced into the large space, and the blinds of the floor-to-ceiling windows rolled up automatically. By the time she'd logged in, the office was bathed in sunlight.

A thick, red, round carpet, ergonomic chairs that looked like they'd been borrowed from a spaceship, plants in every corner, a large painting on one of her walls, and a lit-up statue of a fairy pouring water into a vase of lilies on the other one. This was her domain. A lot more personal than her apartment—she felt comfortable here.

Her fists unclenched. While the email had been sent from Edmund Ashworth the Second's email address, it was signed "Jennifer Vogan, Personal Assistant."

She could have been pissed that the man

hadn't even bothered to email her himself, but she was just glad that she didn't have to put up with his condescending bullshit. Jennifer Vogan was considerably more friendly and professional.

"Dear Ms. Hall,

I hope this email finds you well.

Mr. Ashworth is currently in the city for a short amount of time, for personal reasons, and hopes that he may be able to set up a meeting with Desmond King. I took the liberty of sending this request to the board of King Industries, and as you have been in touch with Mr. Ashworth in the past about this matter, I thought it best to inform you, and copy you in on my email.

Kind regards,

Jennifer."

Hester smirked. Clever girl. She was strong-arming her and serving it up with a side of flowers and syrupy sweetness. If Hes had acted without the consent or knowledge of her boss, she'd be a sweaty mess right now, and move heaven and earth to set up the meeting.

Instead, she grabbed her phone and dialed a familiar number.

"Hestie!" Callum said. "I was waiting till nine to call you. Foolish of me. I see you've been naughty again, crushing the hopes and dreams of proud men all across the globe."

She laughed. "I guess you've seen the request. I should hope that Ashworth's hopes and dreams don't revolve around a harbor. That'd be sad if they did."

"Hey, I don't judge; whatever floats his boat. I pulled the conversation up for a laugh. Shit, what an asshole."

"You're telling me." She rolled her eyes. "Listen, Des won't see anyone right now; maybe you can meet him?"

Hester guessed that while a dick like Edmund Ashworth the Second wouldn't speak to a female nobody, he'd probably readily accept Callum King as a substitute.

"I could," Cal said, musing. "And I will if you want me to. But I'm not inclined to pacify a man like him. The harbor is a King Construction property, and King Construction is currently in your hands. I say we make him go to you. Or we don't sell it. It's making a profit, isn't it?"

She smiled. "Thanks, Cal. I just figured we might want to play nice, given the weight of his wallet and his influence."

"Whatever. Ashworth is all about land development. K.C. is the only part of our enterprise that could interact with him. If he wants to have a relationship with it, he needs to go through you. Especially if you survive the year."

She beamed. "Nine months to go. Still not resigning."

Three months ago, right before starting his paternity leave, Desmond came to her office with an insane proposal.

"You've shadowed me for half a decade. You have the knowledge, connections to run this show, and you also have my trust. I'm a husband, and I'm going to be a father. I won't pull the kind of hours I was doing until now ever again, even after Ryn gives birth. So, here's the deal. I'm leaving you in charge for a year; my brothers and I are a phone call away, you'll have every resource you need. If you can handle it, we'll share the responsibilities when I come back."

She hadn't really understood what he meant, until he added, "With you as COO."

It had been an entire quarter and she didn't think it had hit home yet. Her, Hester Nobody, an orphan no one had wanted, a kid no one played with, the boring teenager with glasses, the prudish college girl who didn't attend parties. COO of King Tech and King Construction.

The very thought made her dizzy.

"And you won't resign," said Cal. "Not in your nature. All right, I'll email poor Jennifer and send her back your way."

CHAPTER 3

She was kidding, right? She must be kidding. There was no way that this was the answer from King Enterprise's board.

"Read the reply, word for word," he said to his assistant.

"'Dear Ms. Vogan,

Please relay my thanks to your employer for his interest in our property; however, I regret to inform you that my brother, Desmond King, is currently unavailable. As the harbor you're interested in falls under the umbrella of King Construction, you will need to directly contact them. I'm attaching the direct contact details of the executive currently in charge—'"

Jennifer lifted her head and winced. "It's a new number and email address, but he's written Hester Hall's name. The reply is signed by Callum King himself."

Ed's fist clenched.

"Dammit."

"I've taken the liberty of asking around about King Industries, and Ms. Hall, while you were in your meeting, sir."

One of Edmund's eyebrows crooked; the assistant might not be completely useless after all.

"Well?"

"It is my understanding that anyone currently in business with Desmond King is contacting him through Hester Hall. He has taken an undetermined leave of absence, between the upcoming elections and his wife's pregnancy."

Shit. "Then who's taking care of his business, his brothers? The board?" he asked.

When he'd enquired about the Kings, he'd been told that each specific brother was in charge of one or several of their businesses, and that they didn't trip on each other's toes, hence why he'd gone through Desmond, who owned King Construction.

"My understanding is that it's mostly ruled by Hester Hall."

He was going to get a headache. "She's his secretary."

"Not quite. According to my research, she's the highest paid employee in King Industries, second only to the King brothers themselves. It is my understanding that she's a vice president of sorts. Without the formal title."

Well, that certainly changed things. Edmund ruminated on the new piece of information, making a mental note to fire whoever had done the primary findings about King Industries.

He cursed out loud. Damn sexism. If he'd read "vice president" under her name in their email correspondence, he would have acted very differently.

"Shit. We're going to have to smooth things

over with her. Contact her and set up a meeting. Somewhere nice; block a good hour of my time."

He wanted a piece of property that wasn't for sale; that meant that he was in need of her, not the other way around. Ed was all for a hostile takeover, but deals like these needed a different approach. He should have flattered, cajoled, and seduced.

"Continue asking around; I want everything there is to know about Hester Hall by tomorrow."

"Certainly, sir."

Edmund eyed Jennifer curiously. First impressions weren't always accurate, apparently.

"Good job today."

Visibly surprised, she beamed.

"David, take Ms. Vogan wherever she wants to go before clocking out," he told his driver, before getting out of the car.

He checked his watch; he was a little early.

A lesser man might have postponed further unpleasantness until the next day. After the last twenty-four hours, he deserved some rest. Ed hadn't slept since Saturday night; he was restless, exhausted, and jetlagged. But he also was an Ashworth, and Ashworths didn't let discomfort keep them from doing what they had to do.

He walked into the lobby of the hotel his secretary always booked, and talked to reception. "Ed Ashworth. Have the Trents arrived?"

The receptionist smiled. "Certainly, sir. They've been shown to a conference room on the second floor. We've also received a number of suits for you; they've been brought up to your room."

"Excellent."

"Hugo can show you to the conference room...."

"No need. The sun room or the blue room?"

"The sun room, sir. Should we call for refreshments?"

He shook his head. "That won't be necessary. We won't be long. If you could send a steak to my room in half an hour, I'd be grateful. Blue cheese on the chips."

"Of course, sir."

"Cheesy chips? That's on the menu?" a bewildered voice asked right behind him.

Edmund turned, mildly irritated at being interrupted.

One glance at the woman and all annoyance fled out the window.

Holy shit.

She wore a cream suit, skirt, and blazer, very well cut and fitted around her delightful curves. Her red plump heels were the exact color of her lipstick, and her hair was tied in a severe ponytail at the top of her head. The professional attire had no right to be quite so appealing. Taking her in from head to toes, Edmund itched to ask if she wanted to join him and share his chips. But he knew he was likely to fall asleep before he had a chance to find out what was under any of her clothes, so he didn't bother.

"No, but they have chips, and they have cheese."

The beautiful blonde smiled secretively, like she'd just told herself a private joke. Ed's relatives were waiting upstairs, and he desperately needed food, then sleep. He didn't have time to find out what amused total strangers.

"Something I missed?" he asked her.

"Nothing. You just remind me of my boss."

Ed chuckled. "How so? It can't just be the receding hairline."

She beamed. "No, just the belief that the world should and would bend to your will if you only demand it."

"Because I asked for cheese on my chips?"

"Because you asked for something that's not on the menu, and took it for granted that it would be available for you."

"Which it is," he challenged.

He could have been irked by her assumptions, and her accusations, but the woman only succeeded in intriguing him. He wasn't used to being talked to like that by anyone but his family. Cici and his mother did call him out on his shit; his granddad had, too. That was about it.

"Which it is," the spitfire repeated.

"Miss? May I help you?"

The reception had opened a second counter. The woman stepped forward.

"I have a meeting at five with William Slate."

"Of course. Mr. Slate is expecting you. If you'd follow me, Ms. Hall."

"Call me Hester."

CHAPTER 4

Ed didn't recall a time when he'd been more distracted. He couldn't afford to be. Distractions were dangerous when dealing with the likes of the Trents.

Hester Hall.

How many Hester Halls could there be in the city?

All right, stupid question. It was NYC, so probably dozens. But how many could be found in an exclusive part of Manhattan, wearing an expensive suit and having a meeting with the likes of William Slate, tech mogul?

Shit.

He'd assumed that the woman would be ancient, because that name was incredibly outdated, right up there with Gertrude.

It wasn't like he could talk. He was Edmund, a name pulled right out of a classic novel. But a woman who looked like her shouldn't be a Hester. She was hot like a Roxy, sensual like a Vivienne, elegant like a Lucinda.

Hester was unique, and now it meant a combination of the three to him.

Ed opened the door of the sun conference room and was pulled out of his musing by the sight of the four people he detested most in this world.

Out of Malcolm's nine siblings, five were still alive; one of them, Cici, hadn't bothered to come for this, completely disinterested in Malcolm's money. She'd show her face at the funeral, and that was that. The other four stood there: Alice, Bernard, Daniela, and Charles.

"Ladies, gentlemen."

He greeted them like strangers, because they were nothing to him.

"I thank you for meeting me on such short notice. I trust it wasn't too much of an inconvenience. I am the executer of Malcolm's will, and I thought it might save some time to state the terms of his legacy to all of you at once. You're, naturally, more than welcome to check with his attorney."

The four vipers exchanged worried glances. They knew that intro couldn't be good for them.

Ed attempted not to feel too smug as he said, "You've all been granted one percent of his company. You'll get dividends quarterly. Malcolm's company will carry on being run by the very competent team he employed. His estate is being donated to various charities—the full list is at the solicitor's. You will need to go and sign your acknowledgment to receive your shares."

"You're joking."

"There's no way he'd do that. No way."

"He was our brother! Our own brother! And he gives us nothing?"

Now, he couldn't help smirking.

"He gives you one percent of his very lucrative business, which should provide you with hundreds of thousands per year."

"That's outrageous! And what did he give you?"

"Yeah, where is the rest of the money? He owned at least sixty percent of his company, anyway."

The corner of Edmund's mouth hiked up. "Well, I don't see how it's any of your business, but there's no harm in telling you—and I'm sure you'll read it when you check, and re-check, the will. My cousin Vanessa, who was so kind as to visit and enquire about Malcolm through his life, has been given five percent. So has Cici. His boyfriend's parents, who've been supportive of him before and after their son's death, have received ten percent. I have been granted twenty percent of his company, which makes me chairman of the board. I have my plate full, so I'll hire a proxy."

"That's absurd!"

"He obviously wasn't in his right mind!"

Edmund tuned his great aunts and uncles out. Who knew four old harpies like them could make so much noise. Feeling light-headed, hungry, and tired, Ed smiled broadly.

"Well, I believe that's the end of the discussion. If you have any queries, you know where the solicitor is."

He turned his heels toward the door.

"Don't you dare leave! You did something to him. You engineered all this! Brainwashed him while he was with you in England..."

"This isn't the end of it!"

Unfortunately, they were right: it wasn't. He still had to put up with them until the funeral, but for tonight, Edmund was done.

He made his way to his penthouse suite and found room service had been delivered. Pulling the plate cloche off the smallest plate, he smiled at seeing a portion of cheesy chips, reminding him of the fiery beauty he'd met downstairs.

He ate one with his fingers before grabbing the tray and carrying it to the low table in front of a large leather chesterfield. The food was gone in under ten minutes. Ed pondered the thought of taking a shower, and opted against it. Instead, he got the letter in his breast pocket out and read it again.

Hey Ed,

If you're reading this, I'm dead. Don't you dare feel sad or sorry for me. I lived the life, in every way, for long, happy years.

I want that for you too. You work too hard, take things too seriously. Man, you'll have white hair before you hit forty if that carries on. Here's something that could help.

Along with the short note dated a year ago, there was a key in the envelope: an old-fashioned metallic key embossed with a K. He examined it closely, frowning. There was no explanation about what it opened at all.

Deciding it was a problem for tomorrow, he crashed on his bed, and fell asleep within instants.

Ed woke up at five. As he'd slept through the night, he might have beaten jetlag for once.

Checking his emails, he was surprised to find a message from Jennifer, sent yesterday around eight in the evening.

She'd attached a file on Hester Hall.

Clicking on it, Edmund stilled. The photo at

the top of the file was indeed of the woman he'd seen the previous afternoon; she wore a long black dress in that picture, and stood next to Desmond King.

Hester Hall, born 23rd of May, 1990, which made her twenty-eight. She'd finished high school in 2004, at age fourteen, got accepted to Columbia with a full-ride scholarship. She majored in business, and joined the workforce at eighteen, taking a job way beneath her as a secretary. Edmund guessed that as a kid and a woman, she couldn't find anyone to take her seriously. She changed jobs four times until 2013, when she was employed by the Kings.

Jennifer had listed all of the deals she'd worked on, on behalf of the Kings. Shit. If he'd had that file in front of him when he'd first been in touch with her, he certainly wouldn't have shoved his foot in his mouth.

He thanked his assistant and mused over the situation.

He really should have acted differently.

This year would mark the tenth anniversary of his father's death. Every year close to

Valentine's Day, his mother spiraled dangerously, but the anniversaries were worse.

Forty years ago, Lola had been in Italy, watching the yachts and sailing boats in the harbor, when she met a handsome Italian who owned a schooner called *My Queen* that stayed docked all year round. He'd converted it into a restaurant.

Lola Ashworth never married Roberto, but she'd loved him with all her heart. Edmund wouldn't believe in love if he hadn't seen it with his own eyes throughout his entire childhood.

His mother spoke about that harbor every time they saw each other. How she'd loved walking on the dockyard, watching the Mediterranean Sea, enjoying the fresh air, and, above all, watching the boats.

The owner of the harbor sold to the Kings fifteen years ago. Roberto still owned his schooner; he had it moved to Marseilles. After he passed, like everything else he owned, it went to Lola and Ed. *My Queen* was still serving delicious food on a dock, but it was past time it returned home. The idea had entered Ed's mind a while back, but he'd concentrated on a number of business matters that took precedence. But with Malcolm's illness, and now his death, he'd decided to act now, before it was too late. His mother wasn't very old, she had long years before her, but accidents happened. He didn't want to live with the guilt of knowing he could have done that for her but prioritized a farming project.

He needed that harbor, no matter the cost. Hopefully, Hester Hall would see things his way.

CHAPTER 5

"Good morning, Chris!"

"I have news," Hester's assistant announced excitedly. "Ashworth asked for a meeting."

"He's been asking for a meeting for a month," Hester reminded him, rolling her eyes.

"No, I mean he isn't asking for Desmond. He's asking for you. And being nice about it, too."

Hes whistled, impressed. She got to her own computer and checked said email, finding it perfectly polite and civilized. He'd be glad to meet "at her convenience," now. Did the guy have a split personality?

Mildly intrigued, she made a pleasant and

short reply proposing three different times and venues: today here at the office, Thursday for lunch, or Friday at five. His reply came quickly, accepting the first offer.

"Chris, do you mind pulling info on that guy? Let me know anything of relevance."

"Already done. Thirty-five, running a family firm, hands in various pies, rich, and granddad is a duke. Silver spoon type."

She'd pegged him right from the start. Hester remembered the man she'd met just the previous evening; a tall, handsome, dark-haired guy with a fascinating behind and the most delectable British accent. Another man who could have fit that description to a tee.

"Any clue why he wants that harbor?"

"None. His company focuses on land ownership and development. He has farms all over the globe, including here in the States. A harbor in a small town? It's random."

They'd bought the harbor he wanted because they'd renovated a nearby palazzo a while back; owning the harbor had considerably facilitated their import of materials. Palazzos weren't the sort of places one could touch up using modern materials; the Italians had always been a lavish sort, particularly in the time of the Medici. They'd needed the finest rose marble, antique sculptures from Greece, and transporting that sort of thing was safer by sea than air or roads. The harbor had been going for cheap, and Desmond figured that buying it would be less of a hassle than paying a fee every time their ships docked. The harbor ran itself with no interference from them, turning in a small profit, and it was simply too inconsequential to have thought of spending time looking for a buyer.

What could a man like Edmund Ashworth want with it?

Hester was intrigued for all of ten minutes. Then, attacking her work for the day, she put it out of her mind; she'd find out soon enough.

The day passed in a blur; the development team of King Tech was ready to present a new product to the board, so they were abuzz with energy and required all of Hes's attention. In the meantime, King Construction was celebrating their twelve-year anniversary and asking Hes to extend their considerable budget or contact a venue they couldn't book.

She was being torn in two, as was her norm. Chris kept her supplied with coffee and reminded her of any engagements fifteen minutes before they happened, allowing her to retain her sanity.

"Hes? The front desk gave me the heads up. Ashworth is on his way."

Hester glanced at the clock on her laptop and frowned, keeping up with the conversation she was having on the phone.

"Excuse me one second, Frank." To Chris, she mouthed, "Make him wait."

Edmund was twenty minutes early. Shit, who even did that in business?

Returning to her call, she said, "Sorry, I had a scheduling mishap. Carry on."

Frank wanted Desmond to sit in on the board meeting when he presented his product, of course; she had to placate him, explaining why it wasn't possible at the moment. Designers were very much like artists when it came to their creations: proud and incapable of understanding the fact that they weren't the absolute priority of everyone else in the business. Hester knew she had to play nice simply because the man was a genius. If she offended him and he resigned on a whim, she could kiss her promotion goodbye.

Their conversation ran over by five minutes. She found herself smirking when she checked the time again. Four past three. She'd made the proud Brit wait.

Using the internal messaging system, she let Chris know that she was ready to receive him. A moment later, her eyes widened and her jaw dropped as she watched a dark-haired, green-eyed, tall, handsome man stride confidently inside her office.

The guy from yesterday.

"Mr. Cheesy Chips," she said out loud.

Edmund Ashworth smiled, no surprise in his expression. Of course. He'd heard her name the previous day.

"The one and only," he replied, taking a seat in front of her without being invited. "That's a lovely office. And with a view."

Small talk. She could do that. "Yes, I love the city."

"Do you?" he asked. "With the traffic, the skyscrapers, the pollution..."

"We can't all own castles and hectares of land in Austen country."

"Just a house," Edmund replied. "The castle is in ruins and the manor belongs to Uncle Marvin."

She had to laugh. "Let me guess. A windy, remote moorland farmhouse."

"Ah! The lady believes me to be despicable enough to reside in *Wuthering Heights*. Am I Heathcliff or Catherine in that scenario, I wonder?"

"That remains to be determined."

“I've always felt a kinship to that poor fellow. '*If you ever looked at me once with what I know is in you, I would be your slave*,'” he quoted effortlessly.

If Edmund was endeavoring to make her forget her first impression of him, it was working.

"A fan of the classics?" she asked, reluctantly impressed.

"Not at all. Give me a good Stephen King any day. But if you'd met my grandmother, you'd understand why I can quote Bronte, Austen, Shakespeare, Dickens, and all that lot."

Still, he was a reader, unlike practically every man she knew.

A very handsome, perfectly charming reader with a lovely smile.

Shit. He was trying to make himself look amiable, and she was falling for it, hook, line, and sinker.

"We're very much off subject. We have a harbor to discuss, I believe."

"Indeed, we do. I want it, you own it. Name your price, and we can begin negotiating."

Hester couldn't help herself; she grinned.

"Mr. Ashworth—"

"Ed."

"Ed, then. We purchased that harbor because it's a few miles north of Venice, and it's deep enough to dock a larger ship. The location has been extremely useful in the past, and should we purchase property in the area again, we may need it. Price isn't the only thing we'll need to discuss."

"Future commercial use?" he asked, a brow raised.

"Yes."

"Ah. To be entirely honest, I intend to purchase it for personal purposes, and I don't intend to allow large vessels to dock there in the future. But I am willing to pay a lot of money, enough for you to buy another harbor —a better harbor, larger, closer to Venice."

Hester's brows hit her hairline. It made absolutely no sense.

"Why?"

The man laughed. "If I told you, you wouldn't believe me."

"Try me," she replied.

Ed observed her closely without a word.

"You're not getting that harbor unless I know what you're going to do with it, Mr."—she caught herself in time—"Ed."

He laughed. "All right. But I'm about to give you a sob story, and you're going to think I'm just giving you the sob story to get the harbor. Which, of course, is entirely accurate. It doesn't change the fact that the sob story is, in fact, true."

"I'm fairly confident that you could have explained what's going on in fewer words."

Ed laughed and looked around her office. "Is there anything to drink around here? I just came out of the most tedious appointment with some relatives. If we're going to discuss this now, I'd rather do it with Scotch."

Rolling her eyes, she sent a message to Chris, asking him to come in. Her assistant popped his head in instants later.

"Do you mind stealing Desmond's Scotch for me? Just one glass."

"The boss's stash?" Edmund whistled, impressed.

"He won't mind."

"But I couldn't possibly drink by myself."

"You'll have to. I can't stand Scotch."

Ed smiled like he relished every "no" coming out of her mouth. She knew his kind. He was taking it as a challenge.

Chris came back shortly with a crystal bottle of amber liquid and a delicate glass.

"Rock, water, sir?" he asked.

Edmund noted, "The man knows his Scotch."

Chris shrugged. "I worked as a bartender to put myself through school. Sorry to say I'm with Hes on this one. Whiskey is gross."

He sighed dramatically. "I'm surrounded by philistines."

"At least there're no sycophants in this room," Hester retorted.

"I'm good without water, or ice, man. It'd be a crime to ruin such a good Scotch. Your boss has great taste."

She let Edmund take a sip and moan appreciatively before prompting, "Well?"

"Well," he said, "it all starts with a British lady on a holiday to Italy, walking in a harbor..."

CHAPTER 6

When he was done telling her about his parents, Hester laughed good-heartedly.

"All right. I'll admit it, it's a good story."

"And you don't believe a word of it," he anticipated.

Hester shrugged unapologetically. He couldn't blame her. It was far too romantic and even had a dead father to top it off.

"I see I'm going to have to be convincing."

After checking the time on his phone, he went to his contacts and called his mom, putting the phone call on speaker.

"Eddy!" said Lola cheerfully. "Still alive? I

would have thought the Trents had set a bounty hunter on you by now."

"With what money?" he asked, snorting. "Mama, I need you to indulge me right now. I have a lovely lady with me and I've just told her about how you and Dad met. She thinks I'm bullshitting her; you mind relaying the story?"

But Lola Ashworth wasn't interested in her story right now. "A lady?" she repeated. "And a lovely one who calls you on your bullshit at that? Who is this, Edmund, dear? You know Cici is desperate for great-grandchildren."

He winced as Hester giggled.

"Ah, what a lovely voice."

"Hello, Ms. Ashworth," Hester said. "I'm afraid I'm unlikely to provide those great-grandchildren. But I am rather curious about your meeting with...was it Roberto?"

Lola needed no further prompting. She sighed before sharing her story, with a lot more flourish and details than he had. When she was done, Hester laughed.

"All right. So it seems your son is no liar."

"Eddy? Oh no. He never lies. He will manipulate, threaten, and bully people into having his way, but lying is beneath the Ashworth name."

"Well, I believe that's quite enough of that. Thank you, Mama."

"Will I see you for Cici's birthday?"

"I'll move heaven and earth to make it."

"Wise man. Talk to you soon!"

He hung up and returned his attention to Hester, who was now genuinely smiling. She'd been tense and antagonistic when he'd first walked in; now she'd relaxed.

"Well, see? I wasn't lying."

"No, you were just manipulating me. I should feel flattered there was no threatening or bullying."

Edmund shrugged. "It's business. I'll use whatever tool I must to get what I want."

"I thought the harbor was a personal matter?"

She was never going to let him get the last word.

"Which makes it even more important."

Hester tapped her fingernails on her desk, thinking.

"I'll contact a team, check the area, see how much another harbor suitable for our needs would cost us, and I'll get back to you with a figure by the end of the week."

She got up, extending her hand to invite him to shake it. Edmund remained in his seat, watching her for a beat too long, genuinely confused.

This was a dismissal. She'd decided the conversation was over, and that was that. He couldn't recall ever having been dismissed.

Getting to his feet, he shook her hand.

"Very well, Hester." Inclining his head, he asked, "Old-fashioned name, isn't it?"

"You're one to talk."

Fair point.

"It was my great-grandfather's. Has yours been handed down?"

It was a fairly innocent question, but he saw her eyes flare.

"No, it wasn't."

He'd touched a sore point. A wiser man would have let it drop.

"No?"

"I was left in a church as a baby. I don't know if the nuns, social workers, or someone in the group home named me, but it certainly wasn't handed down. Not all of us are nobility, Mr. Ashworth."

He was still holding her hand.

"Sorry. I blame the size of my feet. Hard not to stick them in my mouth occasionally."

His poor attempt at humor did succeed in making her smile and roll her eyes.

"No harm done. I'll be in touch."

He finally let go of her hand and started walking toward the exit. Thinking better of it, he turned back.

"Doesn't it bother you? Being called an assistant, when you clearly run the show?"

Hester tilted her head.

"It only affects me when I have to deal with men like you, Mr. Ashworth."

"*Ed*," he insisted. "And men like me wouldn't

be quite so hard on you if you had a proper title under your signature. Chairmen don't like to deal with assistants."

No point denying it.

"Fair," she admitted. "But that will cease to be a problem shortly. My running the show, as you call it, is a trial. If I pass it successfully, I'll get a nice shiny title that'll prevent chairmen from acting like sexist pigs."

She definitely wasn't holding back her blows.

"Believe me when I say that I would have acted the exact same way toward a male assistant."

"Fantastic. An equal opportunistic jerk, then." Catching herself right away, she cleared her throat and apologized. "Excuse me. That wasn't professional."

True, but it hadn't bothered him. He didn't want her to be professional. Ruffling her feathers was a delight.

Ed was hesitating between pushing her a little further and inviting her for dinner when his eyes caught something that made him frown and advance toward a side cabinet.

"What is this?" he asked, his fingertip

extending over a set of personalized stationary.

On top of it, there was a stack of large envelopes embossed with an embellishment that struck him as familiar.

Pulling the small metallic key out of his pocket, he compared it to the design. They were exactly the same, with a K on top.

Hester's eyes closed in on the key and she gasped.

"What does this mean?"

She said nothing, her mouth shutting into a determined line.

"My uncle just died and gave me this key. You will tell me what it's for. Does the K stand for King?"

His voice had lost all trace of friendliness now.

Glaring, Hester straightened her spine.

"This has nothing to do with King Construction or King Technology."

"But it has something to do with the Kings?" he prompted again.

She looked away. "I'll get someone to contact you. Now get out."

Fist curled around the key, he itched to ask for more, demand to know what it was all about, but her tone had invited zero argument. Staying now would trespass on her boundaries, something he'd never done to a woman. It wouldn't start today.

"Very well. Looking forward to your email, Hester."

CHAPTER 7

The rest of the day passed in a blur. Hester managed her tasks on autopilot.

She should have known. At first glance, she should have looked at him and realized that he was Tower material.

Hes wanted to punch herself in the face for not seeing it. It wasn't the end of the world; she hadn't embarrassed herself by flirting with Ed or anything. But she'd liked him well enough. Hester never smiled, laughed, or discussed novels with any business associate or friend of the Kings. She'd made an exception because Edmund wasn't acquainted with Desmond, and she'd believed he was different for some reason. Dammit. Of course he wasn't. From this point onward, their interactions were going to be purely professional. No jokes, no stories, and certainly no Bronte. Better yet, there would be no interaction at all. She didn't have to deal with him directly again. They'd discussed the details of the property he wanted to purchase; now it was just a matter of coming up with a number and drawing up a contract. Another team could take over.

Hester realized she was freaking out, but it was for good reason.

She still remembered the first time she'd stepped foot in the Tower. It had terrified her. Not because of the sex; she wasn't a prude, and she wasn't one to judge other people's kinks, but seeing all these rich people indulging in each other's flesh had made her realize that Desmond King and the likes of him weren't just wealthy, they lived in another universe.

There were rooms where celebrities, politicians, and well-known businessmen writhed with models and actresses, for heaven's sake. People like that didn't take women like her seriously; they were just toys, tools for their pleasure, like the whips or manacles they used on their partners.

That early lesson had served her well. Many a time, an acquaintance of the Kings had flirted with Hester, or asked her out. Each time, she'd remembered the Tower, and firmly shot them down. She'd faced enough ridicule and rejection in her childhood and teenage years; as an adult, she was careful to only associate with her peers, people who wouldn't think of her as beneath them.

She was pissed at herself, because not once during the hour she'd spent with Ed in her office had she even thought about the Tower, or thought to keep him at arm's length. All it had taken to forget her principles was a firm ass, a panty-melting smile, and Italiano-British charms.

"Damn him," she muttered bitterly a couple of hours later, when she was done with work for the day.

Checking her calendar for last-minute surprises, she was glad to find it empty of meetings and phone calls. But there was one conversation she couldn't avoid. Firstly, because for what it was worth, she'd promised Ed she would get someone to explain things about the key, and secondly, because Desmond would want to know.

She dialed her boss's cell phone and, when that failed, tried his home. His wife answered on the fourth ring. "Ryn King."

"Hello there. How are you doing?"

"Very well, although I wish you'd kept Desmond out of my face a few more weeks. He won't let me do anything. If it were up to him, he'd strap me to a bed until I pop his kid out."

Hester laughed. She could see that. "Are you surprised?"

"Not in the slightest. I suppose you want to talk to the man?"

"Please, if you don't mind."

Desmond was evidently close by, as he took the phone within instants.

"You used to take a hint when I ignored your calls," he said grumpily.

"I hope I haven't interrupted anything." She winced, imagining just what she might have interrupted. "Sorry, I should have called Cal or Mav."

Generally, she had no problem contacting the two other Kings, but she didn't know them as well as Desmond, and talking to them about the Tower would be too embarrassing for words.

"Never mind. What's the matter?"

She told him about the small key in Ed's possession. "I've only seen four people with one of those before: your brothers, yourself, and Lily. Aren't they the keys to the Tower's front door?"

She didn't think she could have confused it; the design was too specific.

Desmond was silent on the other end of the phone. Then he cursed. "Shit. Malcolm."

Hester was a little lost, but she decided she didn't need to know. "I just figured I should inform you."

The Tower, like all of the King ventures, belonged to all three brothers, but Desmond was the one truly invested in the day-to-day running of things.

"I'm glad you did; thanks, Hes. Do you

happen to know if that man is related to Malcolm Trent? He said the key had come from an uncle, is that right?"

She thought it out for a moment. "I could be wrong, but I think that the Trents were mentioned during our conversation. I can look into it tomorrow."

"No need," said Desmond. "You're not a Tower employee. I'll handle this."

She was ever so grateful to hear that.

Hester walked home and poured herself a gin and tonic and ran a large bubble bath in an attempt to wash away all thoughts of Edmund Ashworth, King Industries, and the Tower. She ordered her food in and read a few chapters of a good fantasy novel before falling asleep.

Hester had always been great at controlling her body, her mind, her thoughts, her likes and dislikes. She did what she wanted to do, and was who she wanted to be. The one thing she had yet to succeed at was controlling her dreams. And so, while she slept, thoughts of Edmund Ashworth, her desk at King Industries, and a dimly lit private room at the

Tower invaded her mind, polluting it with the filthiest dreams she'd ever had.

She woke up panting, wet, and very, very pissed off. Mostly at herself.

CHAPTER 8

Lying down on his bed, Edmund absentmindedly tossed the key in the air and caught it, observing it before tossing it again, until room service arrived at nine on the dot. He stuffed it in his pocket and had eagerly started on his omelet with a side of bacon when someone knocked on his door.

He checked his food, but nothing seemed to be missing at first glance. Slightly irritated at having to abandon his breakfast after just one bite, he headed to the door, and froze.

Ed lifted a brow, watching the man who'd just knocked on his door with a certain degree of amusement and also some suspicion.

“May I come in?” asked a handsome blond guy wearing an impeccable suit, his hair combed and parted.

Ed had spent one month asking to meet Desmond King, without success. He showed a strange little key to his assistant, and a day later, the man himself was in front of his suite.

He stepped aside.

“Please do. I was having breakfast. Shall I call for anything?”

"I'm good, thank you." The man walked in and took in the room with one glance. "Nice suite."

"It is."

"Great. Let's consider the small talk over, shall we?"

Edmund chuckled.

It wasn't the first time he'd met Desmond; they'd come across each other once or twice at a party, but they'd never interacted until now. Ed was suddenly delighted about that. The other guy was too calculating, his cold eyes taking in everything and analyzing it. It was lucky that he was dealing with Hester rather than her boss, after all.

"The key. May I see it?" he asked, ignoring Ed's gesture inviting him to sit.

Straight to the point, then.

Edmund returned to his sofa and took another bite of his food.

"No, I don't think so. Not until you tell me what it is."

The omelet was delicious, although it was sadly not cheesy. Edmund had itched to ask for some cheddar on top, but, remembering the way Hester had criticized him the other day, he'd stopped himself. Ordering off the menu blew. At least he had bacon on the side.

"I'll need to see it to know that for sure," Desmond countered.

Edmund knew that there was a distinct possibility that they might glare at each other until the end of time if he didn't give in.

He pulled the key out of his back pocket and held it up for about ten seconds, ignoring Desmond's outstretched hands.

"There," said Edmund, stuffing it back with his wallet. "You've seen it."

Desmond's jaw tightened.

"Possession is nine-tenths of the law—isn't that the American saying? This stays in my hands."

"You should take better care of it. Put it somewhere safer."

"Oh?" Ed asked.

"Mine is in a safe."

So, Desmond had one of those, did he?

"Tell me what it is, and I'll see that it's suitably guarded."

Desmond started to pace the room, slowly, like a wolf circling an enemy. "So, you're Malcolm's nephew?"

"That's right."

"It's my understanding that Malcolm had many nieces and nephews. I'm going to have to verify that he gave this to you."

Desmond was starting to get on Ed's nerves.

"We seem to have started on the wrong foot.

You're under the impression you can waltz into my suite and run the show. Now, here's the deal. Given the fact that I have no idea what this thing is, and your assistant blanched when I showed it, I'm guessing it's secret. You either tell me what my uncle gave me, or I'll look into it, and shove everything I find under a journalist's nose for fun. How about that?"

Desmond's eyes were like a snake zeroing in on its prey before pouncing. Remembering that he was in the States, Edmund wondered if the man was going to pull a gun and shoot him or some shit.

Instead, Desmond forced a smile.

"You're right. We did start on the wrong foot."

He lifted a slim folder he held under his left arm and slid it on the small table in front of Edmund.

"What's this?"

"An NDA. Tight and comprehensive. I am going to have to check the provenance and determine that Malcolm gave the key to you, and no one else. But if it all checks out, it makes you a legacy of one of the world's most exclusive clubs. I'll take you there tonight. As long as you sign on the dotted line."

Edmund eyed the stack of papers suspiciously, as he would have any document.

"I'm going to have to get my lawyer to check that."

Desmond lifted a brow. "You don't know your way around an NDA?"

"I do know how to survive in a world of assholes and predators."

Every word had meaning in a contract with a man like King.

"Fair enough. Get it checked. I'll do my work on the key. Meet me in the lobby at eight."

Edmund didn't think he'd ever been told what to do like that, not even by Cici. He didn't think he'd ever disliked a man as quickly and thoroughly as he did Desmond King. They were too similar to get along. Ed was glad they lived on different continents.

"I have something to do tonight," he lied, simply to irritate Desmond.

"Cancel it. We're doing this tonight at eight, or not at all."

Jesus, the guy was a serious piece of work.

"All right. I'll see what I can do."

Thankfully, he wouldn't have too many issues rescheduling his imaginary plans.

CHAPTER 9

Hester wrote to the finance department of K.C. as soon as she got to the office on Wednesday morning, and a report hit her emails by four o'clock on the same day. They'd found five suitable harbors that would work just as well as the one they currently owned; the finance team sent her an estimate of the costs, adding a margin and ten percent on top to make sure that they profited from the transaction.

Hester read the report thoroughly, attempting to be entirely detached about the situation, before calling Claudia, who'd worked on the case.

"Hey. Great findings on the Ashworth deal.

I'm sending you his email. Ask him for four hundred thousand." That was the most expensive option. "You can go as low as two hundred and fifty if he's being stingy. We don't currently need the site, but we certainly don't want to lose money on the transaction."

Claudia didn't think to question it—it was normal protocol with any regular client interested in a King Construction property—but Hester knew that she should have contacted Edmund herself. As he'd pointed out, a man like him didn't deal with middlemen. He might be pissed. Wincing on Claudia's behalf, she told her, "You may want to make it clear that you've been given freedom to approve the sale, by the way. He's a bit of an asshole; if he thinks he isn't talking to someone in charge, he might be rude."

"Charming."

Hester laughed. "He can be when he wants to, which somehow makes it worse. Okay, let me know if you need some help; otherwise, Ashworth is in your hands."

And officially out of Hester's. She smiled smugly, until an hour and a half later, when his name flashed on her phone.

Dammit. Why was he calling her now? Instead of answering, she quickly refreshed her emails to see if Claudia was screaming for help. Nothing. She sighed and picked up.

"Hester Hall."

"Hester. I received the primary documents from your finance team. I'm glad to see they're quite efficient. It looks like I might be able to tie this deal up before going back to the other side of the pond."

"I'm really glad to hear it." Really. "Can I do anything for you in the meantime, Mr. Ashworth?"

"Mr. Ashworth is my uncle, Hester. And I was actually wondering, now that you've shoved me on someone else's desk, whether you'd like to go for a drink?"

She remained entirely silent, mouth hanging open, brain paused. No. The answer was "thanks, but no thanks." Why the hell wasn't she saying it, then?

"Still there, Hester?"

"Yes. A drink?" she repeated numbly.

"That's right. No Scotch, that's a promise.

Maybe some fancy cocktails or beer; your call. Maybe even dinner after. You know..."

She did know. Edmund fucking Ashworth was making a pass at her. There wasn't a version of this where she didn't end up legs spread in his hotel room if she said yes.

The problem was that she wasn't entirely against that development.

"I—I don't fraternize with clients, Edmund. Sorry."

There, she'd opened her mouth and said the right thing. Hester was incredibly proud of herself.

"I'm hardly a client—not of King Construction, or King Tech for that matter. You just happened to own a harbor I wanted. Come on. If you didn't want to, you would have said no about seventy-four seconds ago."

She bit her lip. "I can't."

"Again, that's not exactly a no. Nor do I hear a clear, 'I don't want to.' How about you tell me why you can't, and I convince you otherwise?"

"Because you're rude, high-handed, and I do

my best to not interact with people like that in my free time."

The insult made him laugh. "Still not a no, I see."

He was right, dammit. Her brain was messing with her, flashing some images from her dreams of the previous night. And then, she remembered the exact shape of his ass. Dammit.

It had been a long time since she'd had a chance to let her hair down and have some fun. For all his faults, Ed came with one undeniable benefit: he lived abroad, all the way in England. She wouldn't see him again after that "drink."

"Come on, Hester. Give me a chance to apologize for the rudeness, and the high-handedness."

Another call was trying to get through; the vibration of her phone pulled her out of her reverie. "It's not five o'clock yet; I have a job, you know. And someone is trying to call me, about work. Goodbye, Ed."

"Got it. I'll call after five."

He hung up before she could tell him not to bother.

Shaking her head, Hester answered her second phone call and got back to work. At five, she found herself glancing at her phone, half expecting it to ring immediately. So, of course, it didn't.

She remained at work for another hour to tie some ends for K.T., knowing Frank would have a heart attack if the details of his Friday morning presentation weren't finalized soon. Catering had been ordered by Chris, she made sure to check that there were various options for fussy eaters, and she called each member of the board to check if they'd make it. She knew Desmond wasn't going to show his face, but she emailed him nonetheless—and copied Frank in on that message so he knew she'd bothered to inform the boss. At six, she stretched her back and logged off from her computer, satisfied.

She headed downstairs, waving at the security guy as she crossed the lobby.

"Have a good evening, Jack."

"Excuse me, Ms. Hall? I have something for

you. I would have called if I'd known you were still in the building."

That wasn't exceptional at this time; the admins stopped bringing the mail and couriers at four, unless it was an express. She approached his desk, her eyes widening as he pulled a large yellow basket from the floor. There was a potted plant, small bottles of gin, vodka, brandy, rum, and a bar of chocolate, all wrapped in transparent paper with a big cream ribbon.

Her mouth watered. Hester wasn't one to spend an excessive amount of money on herself; she only got good stuff like those Belgian chocolates around her birthday.

"There was no card, I'm afraid—I checked. It didn't come from a courier. A man just came and said it was for you. I scanned it for dangerous items."

"Don't worry about it. I know who it's from."

"You do?" Jack seemed relieved. "Oh, good. Pamela from Knight Security had a stalker for a while; I hoped it wouldn't be anything like that."

Hester winced. Hopefully not. She'd assumed the package had come from

Edmund, but now she realized she had to check. It could have been anyone, and some sicko could have laced the chocolate with something nasty.

If she wanted to try the chocolate, she had no choice: she had to call a certain irritating British businessman.

Well played, Edmund. Well played.

CHAPTER 10

She called later than he would have thought she would, but she called nonetheless.

"Hester. A pleasure. Are you off the clock now?"

"Obviously. Did you send me alcohol and chocolate?"

Like her boss, she wasn't into beating around the bush.

"Depends. Would I be in trouble if I had?"

"Women have evolved beyond falling for gifts and flattery," she replied hotly. "But I also happen to really like chocolate, so I'm keeping it."

He'd expected complaints and objections rather than a thank you, so he just laughed. "I certainly didn't intend to demand it back."

"Well, good." After a pause, she said, "About that drink..."

"Friday?"

"I'm busy on Fridays."

"Saturday, then. Six o'clock. I can pick you up."

"Why would you? No one drives in the city."

She still hadn't said no, or yes, for that matter.

"Because that's the gentlemanly thing to do."

"I can pick myself up. Ed, has Desmond been in touch? About the key."

He wondered why her voice had suddenly changed. Gone was her teasing, daring tone that made it clear she was smiling on the other end of the phone. There was a certain tension now.

"As a matter of fact, he has."

"Oh. And...has he shown you around yet?"

The mystery surrounding that stupid little

key was killing him. What the hell was it all about, and why did Hester sound so apprehensive when it was brought up?

"He's taking me on a date in a couple of hours. What does it have to do with anything?"

She snorted. "All right, how about you go have fun with Desmond tonight, and you call me tomorrow about that drink."

He paused. "You're under the impression that Desmond will put me off you. You give your boss too much credit. I don't even like the guy."

Now it was her turn to laugh. "Of course you don't. You're way too much like him; you were bound to clash."

She wasn't wrong.

"I don't think Desmond will put you off me. I think Desmond will show you a better way to spend your time in this lovely city. Tomorrow. And don't worry. I'm not expecting a call."

She hung up without another word, leaving him certain of one thing.

No matter what, he was going to call her the next day.

Edmund had dinner in the restaurant downstairs all the while emailing the members of his family who mattered to him. Malcolm's funeral was set for the following Tuesday; he knew his uncle, mother, and Cici would make it. His cousin Vanessa McNamara was quick to confirm that she'd travel up from DC for it. No surprise there. No one else from her side of the family sent anything.

His dessert had just arrived when a familiar figure entered the restaurant, a stunning, tall, wild-haired woman on his arm. Desmond's companion was a mixed-race beauty with a stunning smile. She also happened to be very pregnant.

They spotted him and headed to his table, Desmond grave and the woman sweet and welcoming.

"Hello there. That looks good." Her eyes were on his poire belle helene as she sat in an empty seat in front of him.

Remembering when Gabriella from accounting had been about six months pregnant like that woman, Edmund slid his dessert in front of her, lifting his hand to call a waiter. "Can I have another one of these? Desmond, anything?"

"I'm good, thank you. Ryn, Edmund Ashworth. Edmund, my wife, Kathryn."

"Delighted," he said, quite honestly.

Her presence was considerably improving the atmosphere; for one, Desmond didn't look like he was about to explode. Ed realized that that morning might have been more about Desmond's impatience to get back to his pregnant wife than anything else. Maybe, just maybe, the bloke wasn't a complete asshole. Jury was still out on that.

"Des was telling me about the key."

"Yeah? That makes one of us. I still have no clue what it does."

Ryn glared at her husband. "Were you being —well, you?"

Desmond chuckled. "I couldn't explain things until checking with the lawyer and after he'd signed an NDA. You know how things work."

"Yeah, about that."

He looked through a suitcase at his feet and got the document out. "All signed. I trust you called my uncle's lawyer?"

"Indeed, all clear. As soon as you're done with dessert, we can head over and get talking."

Edmund turned to Ryn. "Is all the secrecy really necessary, or does he just get off on it?"

She chuckled between bites of pear. "A little bit of this and that. Long story short, he runs a very secret club. Your uncle was one of the founding members; doesn't own stock or anything, but his initial donation started the place, so he had a membership for life, transferable upon death. That makes you a legacy. The key is mostly symbolic. It does open the front door, but there's also a bunch of other locks and whatnot."

Well, now he was intrigued.

"Wait, are we talking religious fanatics here?"

Ryn seemed to find the idea hilarious; even Desmond cracked a smile.

"No, quite the opposite. We won't take you to church, although I can't promise there won't be some worshipping by the end of the night."

Her tone was so very warm and suggestive, Ed would have thought she was hitting on him, if she hadn't been sitting right next to her adoring husband.

His pear arrived shortly, and he ate it in a few bites, quite eager to get going now.

CHAPTER 11

Ed couldn't believe his eyes. Holy shit. How could he have lived thirty-five years on this planct without stepping into the Tower? He felt cheated out of an essential experience.

He'd gone to private clubs, and sexy clubs, too—there were plenty of those in the UK—but never had he seen a place quite like this. It wasn't just that the building itself was the latest tech, with state-of-the-art security, or the fact that everyone he came across, on every floor, was either a wet dream or a known face anyone would have recognized, from actors to politicians and royalty.

"My uncle was part of this?" he asked, bewildered.

"Yeah, there're plenty of gay and bisexual members. He met his boyfriend here—they didn't attend very often in their later years, though."

"I can see why. Not many people over sixty."

"There are some older members. If you check the device I've given you, you'll see the room in front of us is locked to anyone under fifty—you can only go in if accompanied by someone in that age bracket."

Playing with the phone Desmond had handed him when they'd walked in, he found the information about the door—playroom, 50+, current activity: orgy.

Holy fuck.

"Here, let me show you."

Ryn demonstrated how to navigate the building virtually, and pointed out the similar rooms on other floors; there was one locked to people under thirty and over fifty, as well as some which didn't have any age restrictions at all.

So many floors, and there was depravity on every single one.

"There are some rooms available to members for short or longer stays; next time you're in town, you could stay here if you wish, rather than booking a hotel. As a legacy, you have access to every Tower. There's one in London, too."

Fuck. What he would have given to know of this place ten years ago.

"So, what do you think?" said Ryn, beaming enthusiastically.

"It's...great. Really."

And it was. He'd been hard since they'd watched a couple of girls demonstrate paddling downstairs, and he'd honestly had a hard time preventing himself from reaching inside his pants and stroking his dick on the dancefloor, watching bodies in various states of undress swaying, touching, and fucking right there in the middle of the room, and against walls, and on sofas.

Edmund appreciated everything, from the depravity to the safety measures. The device stated when each individual member had been tested for STDs, for Christ's sake. He loved the fact that the members were so well-known; no one was going to run their mouth about what was going on there. The very tight, almost threatening NDA made a lot of sense now.

And yet, this place was making him feel...old. Wrong. What he couldn't help but note was that so very many people here were paired, like Ryn and Desmond; they walked with their spouses, kissed their girlfriends while getting sucked by someone else. This wasn't just mindless, casual sex. He'd entered a lifestyle club, and the majority of the members were in satisfying, longstanding relationships. That only served to remind him that he utterly sucked as a partner.

He hadn't cared through uni—everyone was fucking up. In his late twenties, he still figured he had time to find someone he was serious about. But then, he'd found her. Erica had been perfect: smart, beautiful, with a great sense of humor and incredible tits. She loved sex, which didn't hurt. He'd been twenty-nine when they'd started to date. Edmund had taken over the operations of the Ashworth business two years prior, when his uncle retired. At thirty-one, Ed invested in a piece of land in Austria that ended up being a gold mine, full of resources. The deal doubled their worth in less than a year. From that point onward, taken by a bug, he'd traveled the world and discovered more hidden treasures. He loved developing, mining, planting, extending the reach of his corporation. He loved that a great deal more than he loved Erica, and when she figured it out, she dumped his ass.

He'd tried again, with a woman who understood the deal this time; Anna was an ex-model who'd married a mogul in her early twenties. She'd been divorced for three years, and was enjoying a life of leisure in Brighton. But Ed found that a cold, unfeeling relationship didn't suit him either, so he'd broken up with her a year ago. Since then, he'd come to realize that he had to choose between a real relationship and his work, and his work was winning.

These people...they seemed to have it all, and then some. He felt lost and confused. How did they manage it?

"He doesn't like it," Ryn said, pouting.

He laughed. "I love this place. It just makes me feel pretty old." And very single.

All of a sudden, he remembered his conversation with Hester earlier.

The words that crossed his mouth surprised even him.

“Hester knows about it. Is she a member?”

Desmond laughed. “Technically. I’ve given her a membership so she can reach me when I’m here, but it’s not her thing.”

Ryn snorted. "You have no idea what Hester's thing is. She just doesn't mix business with pleasure. Ever. I don't think I've ever seen her with her hair down. She makes the rest of us look like slobs."

Ryn was the kind of woman who couldn't look like a slob if she tried, and Edmund told her so.

"You're such a charmer. Come, let's have a drink."

Within half an hour, Edmund decided that Desmond King wasn't an asshole at all, so long as his better half was in the room.

He made his excuses after one drink rather than joining the melee around him. Edmund was hard, and horny as fuck, but the woman he wanted wasn't anywhere in this tower, so he got back to his hotel room and used his hand in the shower, thinking about red lips, large brown eyes, and long blonde hair in a ponytail.

CHAPTER 12

Hester woke up at five, about an hour before her alarm, and started her usual routine. There was a Zumba class on Thursdays; she tried that rather than her normal yoga one and got to the office at eight-thirty, a little later than usual but still a lot earlier than she should have. She spent most of her morning on the phone with Italy to round out the details about the purchase of a new harbor; it looked like they were going to make a decent profit on the deal as the seller was willing to go down to two hundred thousand euros, and Edmund hadn't flinched at four hundred. She winced, feeling a little guilty about profiting quite so much from a guy who just wanted to give his grieving mom a present. She shrugged it off. It was just business, and Edmund could obviously afford it.

By eleven, she was calling his cell.

"Three hundred. We'll just sell the harbor for three hundred thousand dollars, all right?"

Ed laughed on the other side of the line. "Hi, Hester, how are you doing? Yeah, me too. Great day."

"We'll profit plenty enough at three hundred."

"I've already said yes to four and your team has sent me the paperwork."

Dammit. She should have checked with Claudia before calling him. "Oh. Sorry. I was just—I checked on the harbor we're going to buy, and it looked like we sort of screwed you on this deal."

"You can screw me any time. Really."

Well, she'd walked into that one.

"So, Desmond and Ryn took me out last night. That certainly was enlightening. And it explains so much about your twitchiness. You're not into bonds and ropes, I take it?"

She laughed awkwardly. "I was calling for a business matter, Edmund. I'm working."

"You were being a sweetheart and calling to save me money. That counts as a personal call. Take it off your allotted coffee break time or something."

Her nose twitched.

"That's not how this works."

"How does it work, then, Hester?" he asked. "I can follow the rules if I know what they are."

She hadn't expected him to sound quite so considerate.

"I'm working nine to five every weekday. I don't like distractions during those times."

"Even during your lunch breaks?"

"They're generally working lunches, so, yes. Even if I'm eating by myself—I don't like to have my head out of the game during working hours."

"Understandable," Edmund replied. "All right, anything else?"

"I don't like the idea of being seen after hours with a business partner. That's unprofessional."

"No unprofessionalism whatsoever. What else?"

"I have a personal mobile phone. I'd prefer to use that for non-professional interactions."

"Text me from it. Anything else?"

Why was he being so very accommodating all of a sudden?

"That's it."

"All right. Saturday night, my suite. Room service. They have an excellent menu."

"And cheesy chips."

He chuckled on the other end of the line. "And that, too." After a pause, Edmund said, "I've been dreaming about getting you up there all to myself all week, Hester Hall."

She laughed. "Yeah, right. Let's not pretend this is anything more than what it is, Ed. Good fun."

"Yes, I expect we'll have a lot of fun, you and I. Now, I have to get back to work, and so do you. Talk to you after five."

Hester was astonished that Edmund did, in fact, leave her alone until five, and even more shocked that exactly at five o'clock, her generally silent old phone displayed a new text from him.

She unlocked the screen.

"I'm curious. Why did you think I'd lose interest in you after checking out the Tower?"

She rolled her eyes.

"Like that isn't obvious."

"Evidently, it isn't."

He was going to get her to spell it out, wasn't he?

"There are hot models, and actresses, and singers, all after a good time."

"And you believe that you're not as worthy of interest as said hot models, actresses, and singers. My shrink would have a lot to say about that. Fortunately for you, he's not on the continent."

She started to type. *"I don't think that I'm a lesser person. I just know they're a lot more..."*

Her fingers stilled. More what, exactly? She

erased the message, and replaced it with, "*Whatever.*"

"*Defensive. To tell you the truth, I had a thing with an actress once. Never again. She turned me off the entire industry. I'm certain some of them aren't drama queens, but I have PTSD. As soon as I hear 'actress,' I lose my boner. Serious issue.*"

They chatted seamlessly for the rest of the evening, and the following day.

Hester finished at two on Fridays; with Desmond's approval, she spent the afternoon volunteering at a youth club in Brooklyn, close to the group home where she'd spent most of her childhood. Back in the day, she'd spent most of her free time in the street before that club was founded by the neighborhood parents. Now, giving some of her time there was important to her. Desmond used to overwork her, treating her like she was some sort of a robot, and she hadn't complained, because the paycheck was worth it, but sometime around when he started to date Ryn, he stopped to look at Hester's schedule and made modifications. He let her hire her own assistant and considerably lightened her load. He even gave her the flat so close to Knights and Kings to limit her commute.

Hester had always had a knack for math; she tutored some kids until five, when she taught a simple yoga class.

She ignored her phone until seven, and found three messages waiting for her.

"*Another meeting with the family. Joy.*"

"*What are you up to?*"

"*Done for the day.*"

The last one had been sent about an hour ago. She replied, "*I told you I was busy on Fridays.*"

"*Anything fun?*"

"*Volunteering. Honestly, it's rewarding, but between that and a full week at the office, I always crash right after. My bed is beckoning me.*"

"*Lucky bed. Where do you volunteer?*"

She generally felt quite self-conscious when she talked about her upbringing, but Edmund was equally curious about every subject they'd attacked, and he'd never said anything close to judgmental, so she told him about growing up in the city, and the club, and what she did for it now. She even revealed how she and a bunch of the kids she'd grown up with funded a small scholarship they gave to one Brooklyn kid every year. It ate into her income quite a bit, but she pointed out it was tax deductible.

To her surprise, instead of answering by text, Edmund called her for the first time since Thursday midday.

CHAPTER 13

Volunteering. The damn woman was volunteering at a youth center. The cherry on top was that she thought to point out that her financial donations were deductible for tax purposes. Edmund laughed to himself, making a mental note to avoid introducing her to his mom, or Cici for that matter. If they ever met her, they'd get on his case until he got down on one knee and carried her ass off into the sunset. The woman was that fucking perfect.

He started a few texts, but ended up just calling Hester in the end.

"I have a few theories crossing my mind. One involves aliens sending spies mimicking human behavior to blend in. Gotta say, if that's the case, your parasite kinda sucks. Or it could be a sort of Stepford wife scenario, in a business suit rather than an apron."

She laughed on the other end of the line. "Aliens. Wow. I think you missed your calling; you should totally write sci-fi shows."

"Exactly what an alien would say, arguably. Or you could just be an angel."

She shot back, "I sense a terrible pick-up line in the works."

"Don't need one. I've already got a hot date."

Which did, of course, raise one question: why was he talking to her quite so much? It certainly wasn't his usual M.O., but the woman entertained him as much as she attracted him.

"Do you, now? How presumptuous of you. Maybe I'm just after your fries."

"Possible. I'll have to be persuasive in my endeavor to seduce you."

His phone rang, displaying Alice Trent's number.

"I gotta dash. Talk to you later."

"I'll probably be asleep," she replied. "Tomorrow, then."

"Tomorrow," he repeated, before regretfully picking up his aunt's call. "Mrs. Wright-Trent," he said formally, greeting her like the stranger she was. "What can I do for you?"

"You know very well what you can do for us, Edmund. Our lawyer has gone through Malcolm's will. It is outrageous."

"I agree. If I were in his shoes, I certainly wouldn't have been quite so generous with you. Look, you were bigoted, judgmental, and you paid the price. Neither you nor I can change that will."

"A decent man wouldn't keep the majority of the company for himself while the rest of his family gets breadcrumbs!"

He'd had variations of that conversation with the various siblings all week. Sometimes they begged, sometimes they threatened. They always ended up hanging up angrily after a while. Edmund was only indulging them because he needed them to sign their inheritance; the estate was frozen until all major parties signed off on it.

Cici would sign before the funeral; her four

siblings point-blank refused to, for now. Edmund knew they'd crack eventually; if they didn't give in, they couldn't touch their one percent. From what his research showed of their finances, they couldn't afford to drag their heels for too long. They'd lived a lavish life, spending more than they ought to, fully expecting a large pay-off after Malcolm's death. The first quarter of the year would end next week; if they hadn't signed by then, they weren't going to get paid for another three months. Edmund doubted they could afford the wait.

When he'd arrived in NYC, he'd hoped that the matter could be settled as soon as possible. Now, he wished he could slow down time. Get to spend a little more time with a certain enticing blonde he was either calling, texting, or thinking about.

He didn't even know Hester, but he had a feeling he would miss her when he returned home.

Edmund found himself looking through his workload, checking on his schedule for the next few months. A lot of traveling, meetings all around the globe, phone calls. But how much time did he actually need to spend at the office?

He already knew the answer to that. Not much. In England, he spent most of his time at home, away from London; he only had to make it to town once a month, if that. And, in any case, if he worked remotely, who said he couldn't do it from here? London, like the rest of the world, was just a first-class plane ride away. Ed had no issue sleeping on planes; he traveled so often he was used to it. He could stay for a while, get to know her.

Shaking his head to get the ludicrous idea out of his mind, he headed out of the hotel to catch some air. Staying here? In New York? No way. He couldn't imagine living in any city for an extended period of time, and who made major decisions like that after knowing a girl for less than a week?

He was just being stupid.

Finding a small Italian restaurant, Ed ate quietly, reading a book on his phone. He was halfway through his entree when he noticed the woman who was visibly trying to catch his eye from the bar. She was having cocktails with a handful of friends.

She was a beauty, with large breasts and come-to-bed eyes; just his type. Edmund didn't think Hester had large breasts, although he couldn't tell, as he'd only seen her in a suit, quite unlike the dress poured over the brunette with the martini.

She was visibly open to some fun, and Edmund was quite free to accept the invitation, just like he'd been free to play with anyone at the Tower the previous evening.

And exactly like yesterday, he found that he didn't feel like it. No, he was looking forward to Hester Hall, and no one else would do.

Shit. What was wrong with him?

CHAPTER 14

That Saturday, the time passed at a snail's pace. Ed found himself wishing he'd invited Hester for breakfast rather than dinner. He ended up shutting himself in the study of his suite and working; the hours generally flew by when he was immersed in a planting project. Not today. Dammit. He found himself checking his clock a dozen times.

Finally, at six, he called the front desk to advise them to send Hester up to him when she arrived. He also asked them to deliver some champagne at six-thirty, before heading to the shower.

The knock on his door came sooner than he'd expected it, interrupting his shower. He wrapped a towel around his waist and opened the door. Instead of a hotel worker, he was standing in front of a vision. Hell yes. Now he realized just why he hadn't felt a pull toward the brunette in a tight dress the previous night. Hester was in casual clothing, wearing a dark pair of jeans that made her legs look endless and a red top under an open leather jacket. Her blonde hair, instead of being tightly tied at the back of her head, fell in messy curls all around her face. Brunette didn't compare. This woman was everything.

Hester's gaze started on his eyes, dipped to his torso, then his towel, before going back up, slowly. She stepped into his suite.

"You're early."

"And so very glad I am." Her gaze roamed over him, hungry. "All right," she said as she passed by his side. "Consider me convinced."

Edmund closed the door.

"Convinced?" he repeated, still somewhat dazed by her appearance. She was beyond hot today.

"To stay for more than cheesy chips," she elaborated, stepping closer to him and pressing her lips to his torso without raising her head;

they landed right on his collarbone, sending waves of electricity through his skin.

Holy shit. His dick made a tent in the towel, poking her right between the thighs. "Why, hello there."

"Fuck, Hester."

"Please do."

She hooked her index finger around his towel and pulled without looking away from his eyes.

Edmund vaguely wondered if anyone had ever taken control like that, but the next moment, she got to her tiptoes and planted her lips on his. Then, he couldn't think of anything at all, except kissing her again, and again, and again, while his hands touched everything they could reach, pulling clothes off her limbs. Her arms were wrapped around his shoulders, not letting go.

He only came up for air when the doorbell rang again.

Hester chuckled. "Will they go away if we ignore them?"

"Probably not. That'd be the champagne."

She pouted adorably as he retrieved his towel from the floor and grabbed a twenty from his coat close to the door before opening it.

"Thank you, here's your tip. Bye."

Bucket of ice in hand, he closed the door as fast as he could and turned back to find that Hester had finally left the entryway and walked into the suite. She was sitting on the sofa, having shed all of her clothes except for her lingerie. Black lace. Edmund hoped he wasn't drooling.

"You're so fucking sexy," he told her, in the unlikely event that she wasn't aware of that.

"Why, thank you. Now if you wouldn't mind undoing that silly piece of cloth? I'd like to resume my ogling."

He obliged with a laugh, feeling quite good at the way she followed him with her eyes. Edmund took his time, finding flutes, opening the bottle, and pouring them champagne.

He went to her and handed her a flute. Hester took it in her left hand and crooked her finger to beckon him forward with her right one. He took one step, then another one, slowly, to give her a chance to say if he'd misunderstood her. By now he was standing right in front of her on the sofa, his dick at the level of her face. She downed the entire contents of her glass before dropping it on an occasional table, sat at the end of the sofa, and circled his waist with her hands, palming his butt, before wrapping her delightful mouth around his cock and sucking hard.

Ed groaned, all the blood in his brain traveling downward. His dick twitched in her wet hole. Her head went back, she released his length, and her tongue dipped out to tease his tip. She licked the bottom, removing her left hand from his butt cheek to seize his dick, and pumped it up and down as her mouth explored him. In good time, she wrapped him in her mouth again and sucked, blew, slowly, in rhythm with her hand. His balls tightened, and he sucked in air between his teeth, unable to say or think a coherent word.

"I'm..." Shit. "I'm gonna..."

Her pace increased and she sucked harder, faster, her mouth becoming wetter and impossibly hotter. He came with a low, guttural growl he didn't think he'd ever heard.

Holy shit. How had that happened so fucking fast?

His blurry vision slowly focused again. Edmund remembered how the speaking thing was supposed to work. "You're dangerous, Hester."

She laughed, raising her flute. "Where's that bottle? Your balls aren't the only thing that's empty."

He obeyed. Ed was pretty certain he would have obeyed just about any command from her right then. She owned his ass, and she knew it.

He wasn't used to that. Every time he'd had sex in the past, he'd been on top, in control. With her, he'd have to dance to her song. He found that he didn't mind that. At all.

"Yes, mistress. Right away, mistress."

She grinned. Bull's-eye. He'd been right. She loved to play the top.

"Given your taste, I find it...curious that you seem so averse to the Tower."

Hester shrugged. "I don't mind what they do. It's just not my crowd."

Interesting. Instead of asking how so, he returned with the champagne and got to his knees in front of her before pouring her a flute.

She'd kept her shoes on: open-toe heels most women couldn't have walked in. Smiling, he lifted one and kissed the tip of her toe, then her ankle, calf, the insides of her knees.

"May I spread your legs, Hester? May I fuck your pussy with my mouth until you cum on my tongue?"

She took a sip of champagne, feigning thoughtfulness, before saying, "You may. Just don't make me spill my drink. It's a delightful bottle."

She winked and smiled, and he chuckled. Oh yes, he very much liked this game. Edmund wondered what she'd do if he did, in fact, make her spill. He couldn't wait to find out.

CHAPTER 15

Hester couldn't believe Edmund was letting her play with him like that. It wasn't the first time she'd assumed the role of a dom for kicks, but she would have never, in a million years, thought that a man like him would have let her be in control.

He slowly slid her underwear down her thighs and off her shoes before parting her legs. Edmund looked up at her, and kissed her lips once, softly, before dipping his head lower, anchoring his knees on the floor and lifting her legs up in the air to have a good angle. His mouth wrapped around her clit and sucked at it, then his tongue teased it. He moved both of her legs into one of his hands to free his left one, and plunged a finger in her wet folds, curving it as his talented mouth kept kissing her sensitive spot.

Fuck, he was good at this. So very good. She flung her head back and clasped her hand on the sofa to regain her balance, completely forgetting the half-drunk flute of champagne.

Oh shit. Hopefully, the hotel wouldn't charge him a fortune to clean it. Normally, Hester would have apologized; and she would, too, eventually. Not right now, though. Instead, she glared.

"What did I say, Edmund?"

He moved his head from her clit, regretfully. "I wasn't to make you spill your drink. My bad. I suppose you're going to have to punish me."

Shit. "I suppose I will. Stand up."

He got to his feet, giving her the pleasure of another full view of his dick. Even now that it had softened some, it was still a thing of beauty, thick and long. Her insides clenched in anticipation.

Edmund had been modeled after Adonis: he had the perfect torso, defined muscles, and a fine layer of hair she wanted to curl her fingers around.

"Turn around, Edmund."

She had a hard time preventing herself from giggling like a schoolgirl when he obeyed. He was equally magnificent from the back.

"I'm going to spank this delightful ass five times for disobeying me. You will count each blow out loud. Miss one, and I'll add one. Understood?"

"Yes, Hester."

Feeling quite foolish and extremely amused, she raised her hand and slapped the left bun. Her hand rebounded on the taut flesh. Shit, that was a nice ass. She ran her fingers on the reddening sensitive skin, caressing it.

"One."

She repeated the process on the other cheek, and again until he got to five.

"There you go. You can serve me another flute, now."

"Oh, I don't think so." Edmund laughed, turning back to her. His dick was curving upward, completely hard again. "I think you've had your fun now. My turn."

Hester had absolutely nothing against that development. She grinned broadly as he bent down to grab her by the arms and under the knees. He threw her over one of his shoulders and carried her to his room like a heathen. Hester laughed as he threw her on his bed and crawled up to her. She spread her legs. Edmund glanced at her wordless invitation and snorted.

"Yeah, right. You're planning on lying back and thinking of England? Oh, no, sweetheart. A bad girl like you ought to take it like a bitch."

HE PUSHED her waist up and flipped her over until she was lying on her front. Edmund kissed her ass and pulled her hips back so she was on her hands and feet before biting it and slapping it, making her yelp in surprise and look back at him.

"Can dish it but can't take it?"

She rolled her eyes. "I was actually

wondering if your heart was in it. I didn't feel a thing."

Fucking vixen. He drew his hand further back and spanked harder against her skin. This time, she breathed out, and her ass pushed back further against his hand.

"Not your crowd?" he repeated her previous statement. Her perfect ass belonged in the Tower.

She snorted. "Too rich for my blood."

Edmund didn't understand her point at all, but at the moment, he didn't much care about getting to the bottom of it. Not with that round ass wiggling in the air, begging for his cock. He reached out to his bedside table and opened the new box of condoms he'd bought for the occasion, ripping one open with his teeth and rolling it up on his rock-hard erection.

"Look at that slutty pussy pulsing, begging for my cock."

She pushed back until her legs were right against his, his cock above her ass. "Are you going to watch all day? Should I have brought a magazine with—"

She ended her sentence in a grunt as he plunged deep inside her heat, shutting her sassy mouth up for about a second. Then, he withdrew from her pussy and plunged right back in. Her mouth opened again, letting out a moan.

In his thirty-five years on Earth, Edmund might have fucked a good fifty women at least, and it had been over ten years since he'd prided himself on doing it well. He knew when to go maddeningly slow, and increase his speed, pacing himself to inch them both closer to oblivion. All of that knowledge flew right out of his mind. She was so fucking tight and perfect, and her moans and laughs demanded that he keep pounding her harder and harder, until his legs stiffened, protesting against the effort. His balls tightened impossibly; he knew without a doubt that if he hadn't come just half an hour ago, he would have lasted less than three minutes. The previous release allowed him just enough control to keep going until Hester's walls clung around him. She cried out and fell on her stomach. Her release triggered his; he couldn't keep it in anymore. He came, and came, and came, falling right behind her; her pussy wouldn't stop milking him, clasping around him hard as she breathed.

Ed had no clue how long they remained unmoving, panting. He wrapped his arms around her and fell asleep, only to be awoken by his stomach later.

He frowned, finding his bed empty. Following his nose to the lounge area, he found Hester setting up plates of room service on the small table. And cheesy chips.

He stayed back and looked at her until she noticed him standing there.

"Hey, handsome."

Yeah. He was used to it now.

CHAPTER 16

Edmund was glad he'd set their date on Saturday; he had Hester all to himself through the night, as many times as he could muster, and throughout most of the next day. She insisted on leaving late in the middle of Sunday night—apparently she needed sleep before work.

The moment she left, he had to deal with real-life issues. At three a.m. on Sunday night, it was Monday morning in the UK, and the office had plenty of work for him to get through. He slept a few hours and woke up to funeral-arrangement information. Shit, it was tomorrow.

He managed to sort out the technicalities and went to buy a suit around midday, his mind still on the weekend. It would be a long time before he forgot that weekend, or the woman he'd spent it with. Because of the sex, certainly—it wasn't every day he met a switch who seemed up for just about anything under the sun—but also because of her smart mouth, and her laugh that never failed to make him smile along.

What had she said just last week? That it had been nothing more than some good fun. She was right. They'd wanted each other, they'd fucked each other, and that should have been the end of it. Right?

He tied up his workday by three, as it was eight o'clock in the UK, and then, Edmund stared at his phone, feeling strange. He'd had to stop himself from texting or calling all fucking day.

Then he decided to say fuck it to hook-up protocol and just sent a damn text.

"Did you wake up okay?"

He'd purposely contacted Hester on her personal phone, and he didn't expect a reply before the end of the workday, but his phone buzzed not even half an hour later.

"No! I woke up at EIGHT."

She was still typing, according to his phone. Soon, another message flashed on the screen.

"*And anyone who knows me knows that never, ever happens. I'm normally up by six, latest.*"

"*You went home at two in the morning,*" he reminded her.

"*Not the first or last time. My body clock always wakes me up regardless. I made it to work before nine, but a lot later than usual. You're a dangerous distraction, Edmund.*"

She was one to talk.

And so they resumed their friendly conversation as if nothing had happened the previous evening. Ed was a little lost. What was their deal? They were joking and flirting and fucking. She didn't want to be seen outside of his hotel room with him, so he couldn't call it dating, but at the same time, he talked to her way more than with any casual fuckbuddy.

And he cared. He actually gave a damn about the woman. A lot more than he had about Anna, and maybe even Erica.

He ate out in the city and returned home by nine, annoyed to see that his bed had been remade. He lay down on it and found that he could still get a whiff of her scent on the pillow.

Holy shit. Was he really sniffing pillows now? What was wrong with him! He was itching to text Hester, check if she wanted to pop over for round...eleven? He'd lost count. Any other night, he might have. But he was burying his uncle the next day.

~

LOLA AND CICI arrived at dawn; he had his assistant virtually book a room for them, and went to pick them up in person.

"My favorite boy," Cici greeted him, air-kissing both of his cheeks.

He smiled, knowing she meant it. Cici had two nephews, and there was only one she could stand the sight of.

"Mama."

"How have you been, Eddy? And that delightful girl of yours—I hope it's going well."

"Woman, Mom. That's the correct term for adult females."

Lola rolled her eyes. "We're all girls at heart. Your generation just likes to find everything offensive."

He hugged his two favorite women and took them for breakfast. They only stopped at the hotel for half an hour to get changed before heading to the venue where Jennifer had organized the funeral.

The assistant had been quite handy in the end. Ed was going to have to give her a bonus before he returned home.

The funeral wasn't as daunting as he'd believed it might be; they were celebrating a long, prosperous life. That it had ended was sad, he'd miss Malcolm, but his uncle had been suffering toward the end.

The Trents attended with handkerchiefs they didn't need to use, and glared at his back the entire way. Cici grinned, taking his hand in a show of support.

No sooner was the casket underground than the vultures began circling around Cici.

"I suppose you've heard about the peculiar way Malcolm's affairs have been arranged, Narcissia?" Daniela asked, her mouth thin.

"Peculiar?" Cici repeated. "Pardon me, but what exactly is peculiar about Malcolm giving his money to whoever he damn well pleases?"

Her four siblings gasped. "We're all part of his family! It isn't fair to any of our children that *he* should receive the majority of the funds from an estate that came from *our* father."

Ed had heard it all already.

"Listen to me carefully, dears. I shall not repeat myself. You're a bunch of nasty little gremlins and no one with two functional brain cells likes you. You've raised your children to emulate you. They're all just as horrible as the rest of you lot. Malcolm was a good chap, and he hated your guts. The only reason you have anything at all is because of the blood running through your veins. Now, you can stomp your foot and cry about it all day long, but the fact is, you're screwed. You won't get a penny except for what's in the will. *Unless,*" she added, "you sign today. Then, I'll chuck a hundred thousand in each of your pockets; how about that?"

Edmund wished someone had handed him popcorn. He just loved watching his grandmother in action.

Then a deep-rooted unease troubled him.

She had sorted the problem for him; he was sure the Trents would sign before the end of the business day.

Which meant that it was time for him to return to London.

CHAPTER 17

Lola ran a lingerie design boutique firm in Italy; not unlike her son, she was a workaholic, and nothing retained her attention in NYC. Her flight back home was scheduled at nine o'clock on the very same day. Cici had opted for heading to DC to see her granddaughter, and Lola wasn't one to travel alone if she could help it.

"You won't let your mama cross the ocean all by herself, will you?" she pouted. "You said it yourself, you're done here."

Professionally, he was. But leaving NYC quite so fast didn't suit him at all.

"I... Mom, I'm not even headed to Italy; I have to be in London next Monday."

"And you can stay with me until then, no? Please."

He groaned, wishing he'd learned sometime over the last three decades to resist the woman.

"All right. I just have something to sort out first."

It was close to six, so he tried to call Hester twice but was sent to voicemail both times. She was probably working late. Cursing, Ed sent her a message, and headed upstairs to pack his things. He knew better than to arrive late at JFK. Even with a first-class ticket, security was always a nightmare in that airport.

He checked his phone periodically, and his frown deepened as he failed to get an answer. It was so unlike Hester. Maybe she had a conference call to Asia or something? She hadn't mentioned anything like that.

"Passengers of Flight 5896, we have opened the gate. We are now boarding first-class passengers."

That was them. Shit.

Edmund advanced toward the short queue leading to the platform.

"Why the long face, Eddy bear? Is it a deal going sour?"

He did his best to clear his expression, attempting a smile.

Unfortunately, the woman who'd given birth to him knew him too well to fall for it. "Oh dear. That bad. What's going on, Edmund? You're worrying me."

"It's nothing, there's just..."

If he mentioned Hester right now, he knew, without a shadow of a doubt, that Lola would never let it go. Ever. She'd dig until she knew all the details, and she would, for the rest of his days, ask about the mystery woman who managed to make him tick.

A smiling flight attendant greeted him and requested his ticket and passport. Blinking at the documents in his hand, Edmund stilled.

Edmund found that he didn't actually give a damn about his mother's nosiness. It wasn't what mattered right now.

"Look, Mom, I can't do this. I...I have to go. I

can't leave without saying anything, it's just not right."

The flight attendant blinked. His mother's jaw dropped. Ed, who seemed to just realize the meaning of the words that had crossed his lips, put his passport back in his pocket.

"Yeah. I...I have to go back to town." He kissed his mother's forehead. "Call when you land?"

Lola snorted. "Oh, I certainly will. And I want her name, her picture, and all the dirt."

She wrapped her arms around her son's middle and squeezed him tight. "I'm so proud of you, Eddy."

He laughed. "For ditching you?"

"For finding a woman who matters more than your mama. You're growing up."

Was he, now? If Lola knew he'd only met said woman a few days ago, she might think differently. It didn't matter. He knew he'd done the right thing. Right now, his place was in New York City.

She'd gotten out of the office by six, and the last thing she remembered was one blinding headlight, pain on her right side as she hit the ground, then, blankness.

Hester woke up in a white room that felt cold and smelled of detergent.

"Ouch," she said, blinking. Her head felt like someone had hit her with a baseball bat, like Noemi had in seventh grade.

The rest of her body was pretty sour, but nothing compared to her head.

"And she wakes!" said Chris's voice.

She heard it from her right side but couldn't see him because she'd instinctively closed her eyes again. The light hurt less that way.

"What happened?" she asked. "I didn't see a thing."

"Bike messenger. We're suing. The hospital called me; they couldn't find an emergency contact."

That would be because she didn't have one.

"How long have I been out?"

"About an hour or so. Do you want some water?"

She nodded, and winced. Bad idea.

"There you go. Right in front of you."

Eyes still closed, she tentatively moved and found a glass before her lips. She took a sip.

"Thank you."

"You're very welcome. Bear with me, I just need to press that button—the doctor said I should call a nurse when you woke up."

A few minutes later, a doctor forced her to open her eyes and look at a light. She winced through it, and wasn't very surprised when he told her she had a mild concussion.

"You need some rest, and we'll keep you here for observation through the night, all right?"

She wasn't going to argue. All she wanted was to go back to sleep.

Hester tried to eat a little so she could take the painkillers the doctor had prescribed. She found that Jell-O wasn't too much of an effort.

After eating the dessert, she was given pain meds and fell right back to sleep.

It was daylight when she opened her eyes again. Her head wasn't threatening to explode, but the rest of her body felt worse, if possible. Wincing, she sat up on the bed, and her eyes widened.

Edmund was lying against the wall, right in front of her. What was he doing here? She was about to ask, but she had another priority for now.

"Bathroom," she shrieked, getting to her feet and limping to the door to his left. It looked like a bathroom. Double ouch. Now that she was on her feet, she could fully assess the damage. She basically needed to be wrapped in a five-foot-six bandage.

"Easy does it. Here, lean on me."

Ed half-carried her to the toilet before getting out and closing the door to give her some privacy, saying, "I'll call the nurse."

Good. She wanted to see the wonderful nurse and her delicious painkillers again.

She peed for a full two minutes before limping back to the room. Ed helped her back on her bed.

"What are you doing here? How did you know I was..."

"I couldn't get hold of you through the night,

and at the risk of seeming a little crazy around the edges, I ended up calling the office. Your assistant told me he couldn't disclose your location, and it sounded pretty bad, so I called Desmond. He was in DC, but he's flying back up to take care of things at the office while you recover."

Shit. Shit. Shit. For emphasis, she said it out loud. "Shit! Damn messenger."

She was supposed to take care of the company by herself for a year. That asshole might have cost her a promotion to her dream job.

"I concur."

"Was Des very angry?" she asked.

Edmund frowned. "Angry? At the messenger? Yes. So are Callum and Mav. They popped by earlier. Mav says his wife will bring you a change of clothes and some toiletries."

She listened to all of that, visibly surprised.

"I...I really wanted that job."

"For heaven's sake, Hester, you won't lose a damn job because someone knocked you over. They care about you, Hester. All of them." Then, he corrected himself. "All of *us*."

Oh.

She found her nails absolutely fascinating, and there was obviously someone chopping onions in the vicinity right now, because her eyes were watery.

Thankfully, the nurse arrived shortly afterward to give her breakfast and meds. Then the doctor walked in and Edmund excused himself.

"Thanks for coming," she called.

He laughed. "You can't get rid of me that easily. I'm finding some coffee, and I'll be right back here."

CHAPTER 18

The woman was going to drive him insane, he was sure of it. She had no sense of self-worth. None. Suddenly, everything about her made sense.

"Desmond will show you a better way to spend your time." "Not my crowd." "Too rich for my blood." Hester was a diamond who'd somehow deluded herself into thinking she was nothing but a piece of worthless glass.

Ed found a coffee machine, and grimaced at the first sip. Disgusting, but it'd do. He hadn't slept a wink all night, and he couldn't rest until she'd woken up. Fuck. He was so glad he hadn't taken that plane.

Heading back to the room, he found it empty of nurses and doctors.

"What's the verdict?"

"I'm okay. As there's no one at home, they think I should stay here another day and night to make sure the concussion doesn't get worse." She sighed. "I guess that's the problem with not having a roommate anymore."

There was a little color to her cheeks now; she'd been so pale in her sleep.

"You used to have a roommate?"

"Yes, until last year. Then, Ryn moved in with Desmond and he gave me her apartment. It's in the exec building, not far from work. The commute is a lot easier. I don't love it, but, you know, it's free."

Ed laughed. "A pretty good bonus in the city."

She smiled. "I'm saving up to buy my own place outright."

"In Brooklyn?" he guessed.

"Probably. My heart panics at the thought of paying Manhattan rates."

Hard-working, smart, reasonable.

"I just found my phone, by the way. Your last text said you were leaving for Italy?"

He shrugged. "I was."

"Did the flight get canceled?"

He shook his head. "Guess again."

"Business deal you couldn't resist opening up in the city?"

This one made him laugh. "Not quite. But a certain woman didn't answer any of my calls or texts, and leaving without a goodbye didn't feel right."

Her eyes widened. "You're kidding."

Edmund tilted his head. "You know, I was trying to understand why it's so surprising to you when you hear that people care, then I remembered. Is it because of your parents?"

She stilled. "What?"

"You can't believe your boss, who obviously respects the hell out of you, isn't going to punish you for an accident that's entirely not your fault. You can't believe his brother's wife is bringing you clothes. You can't believe I stayed when I got worried about you."

Hester said, "Because Desmond is a very

successful, extremely strict, domineering guy, and I've seen him sack people for one mishap."

"People who have worked their asses off for years? I doubt that."

"And because I don't know Lexi well."

"You're in the hospital, in a horrible green gown, and your clothes were ruined by a biker. She doesn't need to know you to want to bring you clothes. That's basic human decency."

"And *you* are just...we don't know each other that well."

"Yes, and we're getting to know each other. So far, I like everything I hear, everything I see, except that ridiculous lack of confidence. You're it, Hester. You're stunning, intelligent, warm, sexy, incredibly naughty. Any man would be a fool to let that slip by. In fact, I'm questioning the sanity of any single guy who's ever crossed your path, because I don't get why you're still single."

"Why are *you?*" she challenged. "Hot, successful, funny, smart, rich..."

He shrugged. "Because no one made me care."

Until her, anyway.

He didn't say that. He didn't have to.

"I'm staying in the city," Edmund stated. "I mean, I'll have to travel, but I'll be based here for now, unless you don't want me to. I'd like to get to know you."

She opened her mouth, and then closed it before opening it again.

"How hard did my head hit the ground?"

He laughed. "I realize that's not a no, but I'm going to need an actual yes on this. Do you want me to stay?"

Hester's eyes darted up to his, and she watched him for a long time. Finally, she said, "I'd like that."

Good, because he sure as hell didn't intend to let her slip through his fingers. He'd been so fucking worried when he heard that she got in an accident; not just concerned, but downright panicking about losing her so soon. That and Malcolm's death reminded him that life wasn't granted. It might end at any moment, and he didn't want his to amount to nothing more than a list of deals that made him wealthier.

He wasn't letting go of the one woman who'd made him feel.

Not now, not tomorrow, maybe not even the day after that.

EPILOGUE

The damn house was on a hill, and the wind was blowing in every direction when they got there. And it was the most beautiful place on Earth.

Hester had been raised in the city, and she loved it to pieces, but the first time Edmund took her to his home on a weekend, she decided that this was her place to breathe, take a break, smell the air.

She'd raise her children here. She didn't doubt it for a second, and so she told that to the man next to her.

Edmund laughed. "Mama might have a thing or two to say against that. If she had her way, we'd spend all of our free time in Italy."

They normally flew to Venice when they had time to spare. Lola still designed lingerie, but she now did it in the seaside house she'd built on her harbor. She ate at *My Queen* at least once a day now that the boat had come home.

"Welcome home, Mrs. Ashworth."

The End

Next in the series: King of Kings, a novel.

Printed in the USA
CPSIA information can be obtained
at www.ICGtesting.com
LVHW051653100724
785143LV00031B/303

9 781839 840289